THE PONY EXPRESS

Hurry, hurry! Read all about it!

New letter delivery service! Letters from
New York to San Francisco in just thirteen days!

Read all about it!

Come along with Buffalo Biff and Farley's Raiders.

We're headed to the Pony Express!

turn page

Scene 1: Horse Sense

Ruby: Yaw! Giddy up!

Pete: Hi Ruby!

Ruby: Hi Pete!

Pete: You ride like an expert, Ruby!

Biff: Ruby and I started riding when we were very young, Pete.

Pete: I remember when your parents would take you riding. I wish I could ride as well as you and Ruby.

Biff: And that's what brings us to why we brought you out to the stables today, Pete.

Pete: And why would that be, Biff?

Biff: Our next time travel adventure has much to do with horses, so I wanted you to be familiar with them and maybe even get you up on one today.

Pete: Oh no! I'm not getting on a horse!

turn page

Ruby: Why, Pete Picasso, did I hear you say you don't want to ride one of these fine animals?

Pete: I didn't say. Oh, I don't know.

Biff: Relax, Pete. We're not going to make you do anything you don't want to. But it might come in handy.

Ruby: Did Biff tell you where we're going, Pete?

Pete: We didn't get around to that yet, Ruby. I'm still trying to get past this horse thing.

Ruby: Pete, this is Horatio. Horatio, this is Pete.

Pete: How do you do, Horatio.

turn page

Pete:	It's like he knows what I'm saying.
Ruby:	He does Pete. He knows exactly what you're saying. Horses are very smart.
Biff:	Go ahead, pet him, Pete. He won't bite you.
Pete:	Nice Horatio. Good Horatio.
Ruby:	He likes you, Pete!
Pete:	Yes, I guess he does. Hey, this is pretty cool.
Biff:	I guess this would be a good time to tell you where our next time travel adventure will be taking us.
Ruby:	I'm really excited about this, Pete! I hope you'll be excited, too!
Biff:	We're going to visit the Pony Express!

turn page

Pete:	The Pony Express! You mean like, cowboys?
Biff:	That's right!
Pete:	The wild west?
Ruby:	Right again, Pete!
Pete:	Miles and miles of the roughest terrain America has to offer?
Biff:	Right!
Pete:	You mean like, "Got to get the mail to Sacramento on time?"
Ruby:	That pretty well sums it up, big boy.
Pete:	Someone saddle up a horse! I've got to learn how to ride!
Biff:	All right! We're headed to the Pony Express!
All:	Yahoo!

turn page

Scene 2: Preparing The Time Machine

Ruby: You did very well for your first lesson in riding, Pete.

Pete: It wasn't so bad once I made friends with Horatio.

Ruby: That's one of the keys, Pete. You can be friends, but you also have to let the horse know that you are in control.

Pete: I'll learn all that in time.

Biff: You don't have to be an excellent rider for this adventure, Pete. We're just going to observe and learn.

Ruby: But it's good if you know something about riding before we go.

Biff: I'm getting the time machine ready for the trip.

turn page

Ruby: I have my special necklace, which allows me to communicate with animals.

Pete: I have my special bracelet that gives me a great sense of direction. With my bracelet, we can't possibly get lost!

Biff: Farley always has his collar on, which lets us know where he is at all times. And I have my special buffalo horns, which is the key to all of our magical powers.

Ruby: I hope we'll get to see Little Big Dog again.

Pete: We have that great Indian to thank for our special powers, and even time travel.

Ruby: That's right, Pete. Biff's time machine is great, but it's Little Big Dog's magic that supplies the fuel.

Pete: Where are we going first, Biff?

Biff: The first Pony Express rider rode out of St. Joseph, Missouri, April 3rd, 1860. I guess that would be a good place to start.

turn page

Ruby: 1860!

Pete: Wow!

Biff: Fasten yourselves in! We're about to blast off!

Ruby: My necklace is glowing!

Pete: We're glowing all over.

Biff: Hang on everyone! We're going to the Pony Express!

All: Yahoo!

turn page

Scene 3: Time Traveling

Pete: What a thrill! I never get over the thrill of the blast off!

Farley: Ruff! Ruff!

Ruby: Farley agrees with you, Pete.

Pete: How did the Pony Express get its start, Biff?

Biff: William Russell, Alexander Majors, and William Waddell put up two hundred thousand dollars for a more direct mail system.

Pete: Two hundred thousand dollars?

Biff: That's right, Pete. Now, at this point, it took about a month for the U.S. Postal Service to get a letter from New York to California.

Pete: A whole month?

Biff: The mail traveled from New York to California by ocean.

Ruby: They had to travel south from New York, overland across the Isthmus of Panama and then north to California.

Biff: That's exactly right, Ruby!

Pete: No wonder it took so long.

turn page

Ruby: So... these men started a private carrier service, the Pony Express, with the intent to deliver the mail in just thirteen days.

Biff: They bought five hundred first class horses, and set up one hundred ninety relay stations along almost two thousand miles of America's roughest territory.

Pete: Why didn't they just send messages across the country by telegraph?

Ruby: I don't think the telegraph system went that far at that time.

Biff: Right again, Ruby. The telegraph only went as far west as St. Joseph, Missouri.

Pete: Oh, okay. That's why the Pony Express began at St. Joseph.

turn page

Ruby: But the mail traveled from New York to San Francisco.

Biff: Good point Ruby! On March 31st, 1860, the first Pony Express mail was dispatched by train to St. Joseph from Washington and New York.

Pete: By train! I love trains!

Biff: But that's another adventure, another time, Pete. Once the mail arrived in Sacramento, it traveled by steamship on to San Francisco.

Ruby: We're gearing down, Biff. We must be getting close to our destination.

Biff: Pony Express, just ahead!

turn page

Scene 4: The First Send Off

Pete: What are those people doing?

Biff: They've come to see the first Pony Express rider ride off with the mail.

Ruby: Let's get closer so we can read that sign, Biff.

Pete: Wanted. Young, skinny, wiry fellows not over eighteen.

Biff: The riders had to be small and light weight, to allow for the approximately twenty pounds of mail they had to carry.

Ruby: Must be expert riders, willing to risk death daily.

turn page

Biff: As dangerous as the job was, they carried no weapons for defense, as their weapons would only weigh them down.

Pete: They couldn't take much at all.

Biff: However, every Pony Express rider was presented with a full-size copy of the Holy Bible to carry with them on their dangerous journey.

Pete: Orphans preferred.

Ruby: Why orphans?

Biff: There would be no one to long for them if they were killed on the job.

Pete: Killed on the job?

Biff: It is interesting to note that through the entire life of the Pony Express, not one rider was killed on the job.

turn page

25

Pete: Oh, okay. That makes me feel a little better.

Ruby: Wages, twenty-five dollars per week.

Pete: I guess that was a lot of money back then.

Biff: The riders rode through two thousand miles of one hundred twenty degree deserts or snowbound Sierra passes.

Ruby: Not to mention, Indian territory.

Pete: Wow!

turn page

27

Ruby: Here comes the train!

Pete: I love trains!

Ruby: Yes, we know, Pete.

Biff: There it is! The mail comes off the train and goes into the cantinas on the rider's "mochila".

Pete: Mochila! What's a mochila?

Biff: It's a saddle cover with four pockets or cantinas. It slips over the rider's very small light-weight saddle.

turn page

Ruby: Forty-nine letters, five telegrams.

Pete: And a special light-weight edition of the St. Joseph Daily Gazette.

Biff: Letters were written on a thin light-weight paper. The postage however, was bulky and weighed more than the letters.

Ruby: The rider is checking his horse's hooves. Look at how small the horse shoes are.

Biff: Even those had to be reduced in size and weight to make the trip easier for the horse and rider. Well, it's seven o'clock on the evening of April 3rd, 1860.

Pete: So, what does that mean?

Ruby: It means, it's time for this piece of history to begin.

turn page

Scene 5: Follow That Rider

Pete: Follow him, Biff. Is he going to carry the mail all the way to Sacramento?

Ruby: Since the run to Sacramento will be made in only ten days, I doubt that he or the horse could make the trip without some help.

Biff: Many riders are involved. Each rider averages seventy-five miles per run.

Ruby: And they switch horses every ten to fifteen miles.

Pete: This is so exciting! Let's go forward in time and see where he makes his mail transfer.

turn page

Ruby: Look, another horse and rider are waiting for him.

Pete: He dismounts.

Biff: He passes the mochila to his partner.

Ruby: It goes over the fresh horse's saddle.

Pete: The new rider mounts up. And they're off! Flaming Arrow's in the lead as they round the corner!

Ruby: It's not a horse race, Pete.

Pete: Oh, I know. I was just...

Ruby: Getting carried away with yourself?

Pete: Well, maybe just a bit.

turn page

Farley: Rrrr, rrr, rrr, rrr, Ruff! Ruff! Ruff!

Ruby: What is it, Farley?

Farley: Ruff! Ruff!

Ruby: You're right, Farley!

Pete: What's the matter, Ruby?

Ruby: Farley says, the rider dropped a piece of paper!

Biff: A piece of paper? We better move in close and see what it is. I'll use Buffalo Biff's "Magnificent-Maximizing-Magnifying-Ultra-Mighty Monitor" to hone in on it!

turn page

Pete: That's some kind of special monitor alright, Biff.

Ruby: Oh no, it's a piece of mail! He dropped it!

Biff: This could change history!

Pete: How could one letter change history?

Ruby: According to history, all the mail made it from St. Joseph to Sacramento.

Biff: The Pony Express was hailed by many newspapers as being the fastest and most reliable means of mail transportation of the day.

turn page

Ruby: If even one piece of mail is missing, this could mean an early end to the Pony Express.

Pete: Well then, we'll just have to think of something.

Ruby: We have to find a way to get that letter back into the cantina.

Biff: We can't risk being seen by the rider. We would look very strange to him.

Ruby: And we might spook the horse.

Farley: Ruff! Ruff! Ruff!

Pete: What's Farley trying to say, Ruby?

Farley: Ruff!

Ruby: Good idea, Farley!

turn page

Biff: Don't tell me. I think I know what Farley said. The rider wouldn't find it too strange to see a dog, right?

Ruby: Right, Biff?

Biff: We just need to zoom up ahead of him.

Pete: And Farley will distract the rider.

Biff: The rider can't see us if we stay in the time machine. Farley can keep him busy and I'll slip the letter back in the cantina!

Ruby: Sounds like a plan!

turn page

Ruby: Okay, Farley. Do your thing, boy.

Farley: Ruff! Ruff! Ruff!

Rider: Whoa! What the... Well, look at that! Hey fella', what are you doing way out here? I'm a few minutes ahead of schedule... come here, boy. Okay, I'll come there.

Ruby: Here's our chance, Biff.

Biff: Success!

Rider: What's that? Who's there? Could be Indians. Come on boy, you're coming with me. Yah! Giddy up!

turn page

Pete: Uh, was that part of our plan?

Biff: No, it wasn't.

Ruby: What do we do now, Biff?

Biff: We just stay with him!

Ruby: We can't lose Farley, Biff!

Biff: We're not going to lose Farley, Ruby! Don't worry.

turn page

Pete: Stay with him, Biff!

Ruby: Just a little closer. A little closer. I've got him!

Pete: Welcome home, Farley.

Rider: Hey, where'd you go, boy? Yah!

turn page

Scene 6: The Mail Arrives

Ruby: Well, they did it. They carried the mail from St. Joseph to Sacramento in just ten days.

Pete: Through all kinds of territory and sometimes even harsh conditions.

Ruby: Neither snow, nor rain, nor heat, nor gloom of night.

Biff: Actually, that's the unofficial motto of our modern mail service. An ancient Greek historian came up with those words about twenty-five hundred years ago.

Pete: How do you know all this stuff, Biff?

Biff: I love to read! I love to study! I love school!

Ruby: I really enjoyed this adventure, Biff.

Pete: What became of the Pony Express?

Biff: It ended just eighteen months after it began. The telegraph made its way out west and the Pony Express disbanded.

turn page

Ruby: Three hundred eight runs were made each way.

Biff: That equals twenty-four times around the earth!

Pete: Wow!

Ruby: And they delivered thirty-four thousand, seven hundred fifty-three pieces of mail!

Biff: There's a lot more to the Pony Express than we've seen today. It played a big part in the Civil War.

Ruby: In the life of Abraham Lincoln.

Biff: In the lives of Buffalo Bill Cody and Wild Bill Hickock.

Pete: I want to learn more about the Pony Express, Biff.

Biff: It's all at the library, Pete!

turn page

Pete: Where to next, Biff?

Biff: That's one of the exciting things about us, Pete.
          You just never know where our next adventure
          will take us.

Ruby: We're Buffalo Biff and Farley's Raiders!

All: Yahoo!

turn page

Now it's your turn. Fill in the missing lines for Biff, Ruby or Pete, and become one of

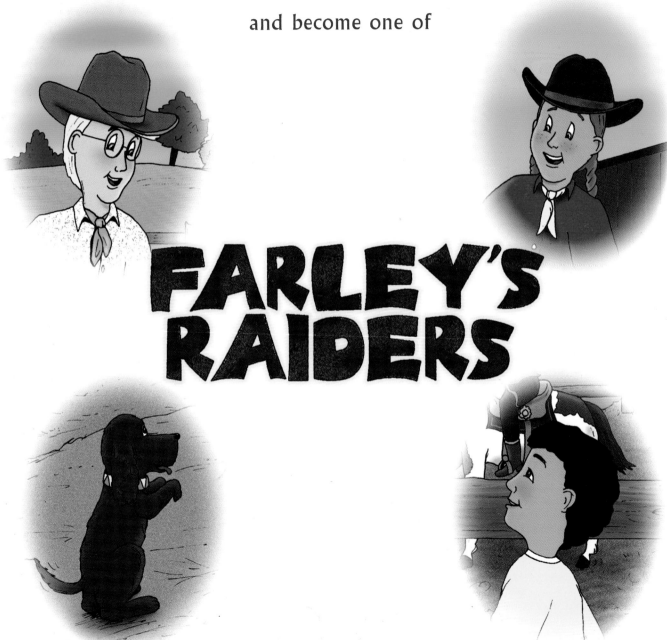

FARLEY'S RAIDERS